This Book Given To:

_____

From

_____

Date

_____

Bilingual Books also available
in the following languages:

Italian   I Miei Cugini, I Miei Amici

Spanish   Mis Primos, Mis Amigos

French   Mes Cousins, Mes Amis

All languages also available
In digital format / E-Book

My Cousins, My Friends

Written By
Diana DelRusso

Ilustrated By
Kimberly Young

My Cousins, My Friends

**Dedicated to everyone
who has special
cousins in their lives.**

My Nana says cousins are like leaves,
that grow on the same tree.

They all might look the same
but they are each a little different.

They come from the same place
in the beginning, like the trunk of a tree.

Over time they spread out
like the branches of the tree.

I have many cousins.
Boy and girl cousins.
I have grown up cousins
and little kid cousins.

Even my Mom's cousins
are my second and third cousins.
That part is tricky.

Nana says those cousins
come from a really big tree
with lots of branches
and colorful leaves.

I'm sure I haven't even
met all of my cousins yet.

Nana says they live all over the country.

Too far for me to see,
like leaves that blew far from their tree.

I don't know all of their names
but I think my Nana does.

Nana says having cousins is like,
having a bunch of best friends forever!

They don't have to know each other
to love each other.

When they do meet they smile and
hug because they feel like they have
always known each other.

I wonder if that's how the leaves feel
When the wind blows them off their branches
And they swirl around and around together.

Maybe that's like a bunch of cousins
visiting each other and making friends.

I wish I was a leaf on a tree that could
blow in the wind and meet all of my
cousins someday, then I would have
a bunch of best friends forever!

Nana says families have reunions
because cousins feel their roots
pulling them home again, like when
the wind blows the scattered leaves
back under their tree.

Nana says maybe their roots are
pulling them home again too.

I don't know about that.
I just like jumping in a pile of leaves
with my cousins, my friends.

The End

About the Author, *Diana DelRusso*

has been writing for over forty years, creating characters and fictional stories.

In 2007, she published her first book, *The Magical Journey*.
In 2008, she published her first Christmas book, *Pages the Book-maker Elf*.
In 2019, she published her second Christmas book in the Pages series, *Pages Awakens the Fireflies*. Also in 2019, she created three story coloring books and plans to create more in the future.
In 2021, she has published *Nana's Precious Kittens* the first book in her Nana's Precious Pets series. Also in 2021, DelRusso has published her first set of bilingual books. *My Cousins, My Friends* is available in English, Italian, French and Spanish.

She has shared her stories with children all over the country; promoting reading and writing with her personal program, Imagination/Creation. She has created multiple fundraising events. With an increasing social media presence, DelRusso continues to share her books with children around the world.

Follow her website for future book release dates, appearances, events and exciting information!

www.dianadelrusso.com

About the

Illustrator,

Kimberly Young

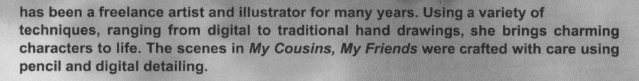

has been a freelance artist and illustrator for many years. Using a variety of techniques, ranging from digital to traditional hand drawings, she brings charming characters to life. The scenes in *My Cousins, My Friends* were crafted with care using pencil and digital detailing.

Since 2002, Kimberly has enjoyed bringing multiple mediums together to create fun and interesting artwork. Her portfolio includes many corporate projects for business purposes, as well as work with screen printers and metal craft. From illustration and mural painting to logo design and packaging, she has had her hand in almost every artistic medium.

Originally from Idaho, Kimberly now travels the world with her family. They have lived and worked in 34 US States and territories, as well as 12 countries. The adventure has included planes, trains, RV's, boats, blizzards, hurricanes and volcanos, with no sign of slowing down. You can see samples of her work and reach out to her by visiting:

www.artisticbynature.com

My Cousins, My Friends
copyright @ 2021 Diana DelRusso
Illustrations by Kimberly Young
Cover design and page layout: Kimberly Young

Names: DelRusso, Diana, author. | Young, Kimberly, illustrator.
Title: My Cousins, My Friends / by Diana DelRusso;
illustrated by Kimberly Young Description: Redlands, CA: Diana DelRusso, 2021.

Summary: A story describing the special bond between cousins, using the leaves of a tree an analogy for cousins in a family. Bilingual book available in Italian, French and Spanish.

Hardcover ISBN: 978-1-7375385-9-2

Paperback ISBN: 978-1-7379793-0-2

E-book ISBN: 978-1-7379793-1-9

Library of Congress Control Number: 2021919311

My Cousins, My Friends

Color a leaf for each of your cousins.
Color the heart for yourself.
or
Write your cousins names in the leaves.
Write your own name in the middle.

Made in the USA
Las Vegas, NV
08 September 2023

77246401R00017